THIS CANDLEWICK BOOK BELONGS TO:

_____

_____

_____

For Aunt Jane, with love
C. D. S.

To Toots and Paka
S. N.

Text copyright © 2002 by Carol Diggory Shields
Illustrations copyright © 2002 by Scott Nash

First paperback edition 2005

The Library of Congress has cataloged
the hardcover edition as follows:

Shields, Carol Diggory.
The bugliest bug / Carol Diggory Shields ;
illustrated by Scott Nash. — 1st ed.
p.   cm.
Summary: All kinds of insects compete to see
who is the bugliest bug of all, but there is a
sinister surprise behind the contest.
ISBN 978-0-7636-0784-5 (hardcover)
[1. Insects—Fiction. 2. Spiders—Fiction.
3. Contests—Fiction. 4. Stories in rhyme.]
I. Nash, Scott, ill.   II. Title.
PZ8.3.S55365 Bu 2002
[E]—dc21   2001025812

ISBN 978-0-7636-2293-0 (paperback)

20 21 22 APS 15 14

Printed in Humen, Dongguan, China

This book was typeset in Alghera.
The illustrations were done in gouache and pencil.

Candlewick Press
99 Dover Street
Somerville, Massachusetts 02144

visit us at www.candlewick.com

THE BUGLiEST BUG

Carol Diggory Shields   illustrated by Scott Nash

CANDLEWICK PRESS

Do you have six legs?
Do you wiggle
or crawl?
Could YOU be
the bugliest bug
of them all?

A contest for insects!

News buzzed through the air.
Bugs slithered and swarmed
    from here and from there.

Down by the pond,
    young Damselfly Dilly
Said, "I'm a plain bug,
    neither clever nor frilly.

"But while I won't win
    I would still like to see
Who the Bugliest Bug
    turns out to be."

Fireflies lit up the stage
with their lights.
Glowworms glowed softly,
a beautiful sight!

A lacy white curtain
hung from the trees
And billowed and swayed
in the warm evening breeze.

The clearing was humming
with bugs of all sizes,
Flittery, jittery,
hoping for prizes.

There were more bugs than Dilly could ever have dreamed,
From tiny no-see-ums to fat termite queens.

Some had great pincers, some had proud horns,
Some looked like branches, or flowers, or thorns.

Dilly crept closer
    as the biggest judge grinned.
"Sweet little bugs,
    let our contest begin!"

"How odd," Dilly thought.
    "Those judges have wings
That are tied to their backs
    with gossamer strings."

Click beetles clacked, and whirligigs whirled,

Crickets sang solo, and swallowtails twirled.

A ladybug curtsied, tumblebugs flipped,

The judges applauded, then licked their lips.

The judges looked shifty,
  so Dilly kept squinting . . .
Then—sure enough—
  she spied their **fangs** glinting!

She yelled, "We've been
flim-flammed,
bamboozled,
distracted.
Those judges aren't insects," she cried. . . .

The big judge hissed softly,
  "Too late for you all—
It's curtain time now."
  And it started to fall.

"Folks," he continued,
  "we liked all your acts,
But we think we will like you
  much better as snacks."

The bugs froze in fear—
  this looked like the end. . . .

But Dilly thought quickly,
    and shouted out, "Friends!
There's only one way to
    get out of this mess—
Each insect must do what
    each insect does best!"

So—"Charge!" yelled a squadron
    of swift soldier flies,
And bombardier beetles
    took to the skies.

Dilly whirred up through
    a hole in the net.
"It's working, it's working!
    We'll beat those creeps yet!"

The army ants marched and

the mantises prayed.

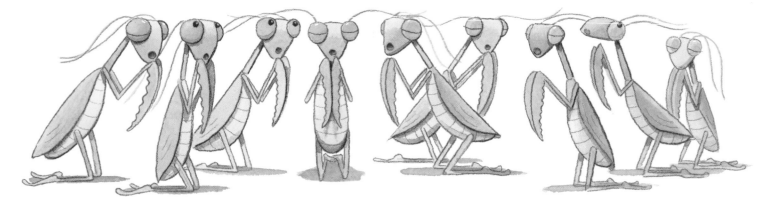

"Keep fighting," called Dilly,
"and don't be afraid!"

Then the stink bugs united, gave off their worst smells.
"P. U., we give up!" the spiders all yelled.

They scuttled away—

"Hurrah!" cried the bugs,
Giving high-sixes and
fuzzy, warm hugs.

The cicada piped up:
"It's time for a speech.
Attention, my friends,"
he said with a screech.

"The contest is over,
    and we have a winner—
Without this young damsel
    we'd all be dinner.

"She might be young and
    she might be small . . .

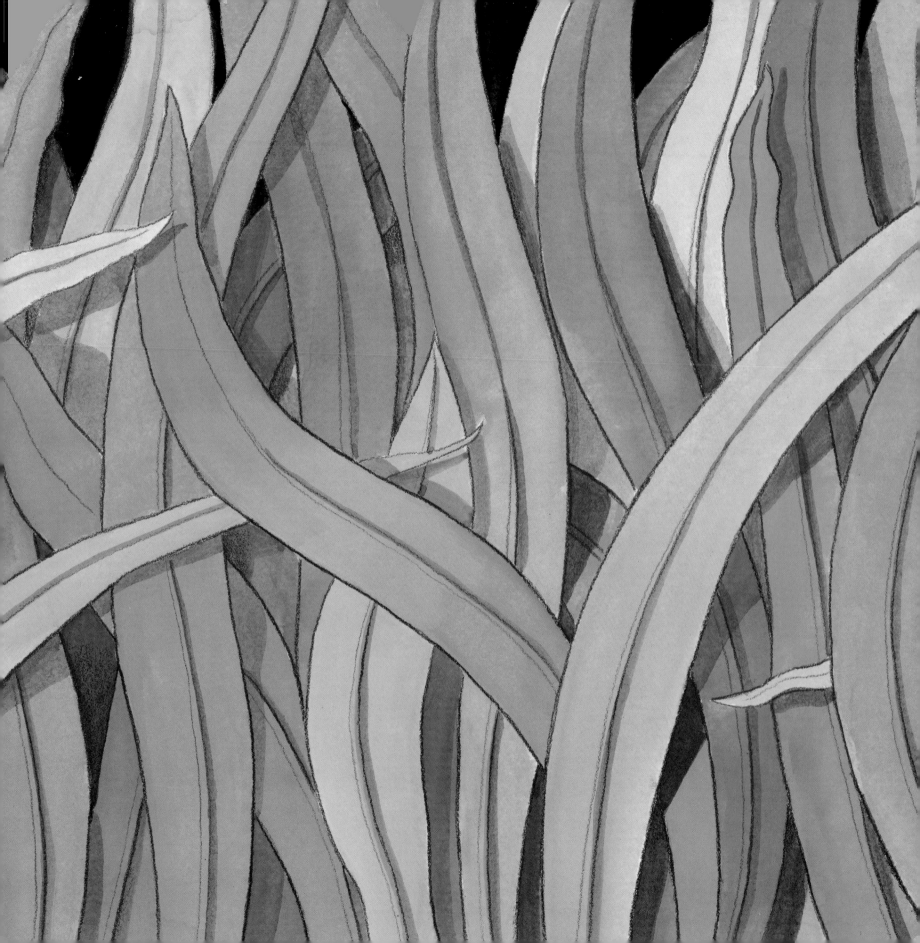

Flying Ant

Order: Hymenoptera, Family: Formicidae

Winged ants, or "flying ants," are responsible for the reproduction of the ant colony.

Flying Ant is a rescue pilot. He has saved ants from being stepped on, swatted, and plucked from picnic baskets.

Cicada

Order: Homoptera, Family: Cicadidae

The adult life of the cicada lasts less than 3 weeks, but in this time, it must emerge from the ground, find a mate, and lay its eggs.

Fran is a karaoke and yodeling champ — she is considered to be the loudest insect in the world.

Damselfly

Order: Odonata, Family: Coenagrionidae

Damselflies have excellent vision because of large compound eyes that allow them to see in all directions.

Dilly the Damselfly is big on bravery. She can fly sideways, forward, backward, and upside down!

Praying Mantis

Order: Mantodea, Family: Mantidae

While mantids may look like they are praying, they are actually hunting!

Praying Mantis manages to juggle motherhood and a career while still making time for yoga. She resides with her 300 babies in a grass hut.

Stink Bug

Order: Hemiptera, Family: Pentatomidae

The triangular-shaped stink bug is named for the smelly fluid it produces to protect itself.

John Stink Bug is the inventor of P.U. Goo, a vile-smelling juice that can be squirted at enemies. He can spray the stinky juice 12 inches!

Stick Bug

Order: Phasmida, Family: Phasmatidae

Stick bugs like to blend in with sticks and leaves during the day and become active at night.

Mr. Stick Bug is believed to be the longest insect in the world. He enjoys pretending to be a stick with his two children, Stretch and Twiggy.

Swallowtail

Order: Lepidoptera, Family: Papilionidae

These butterflies got their name from the long "tails" on their hind wings, which look like the tails of swallows.

Dotty is a pageant favorite. She is an accomplished clogger, yet enjoys any dance that involves floating or twirling.

Tumblebug

Order: Coleoptera, Family: Scarabaeinae

By rolling manure into balls and burying them underground, tumblebugs help clean, prevent disease, and fertilize growing plants.

Also known as Dung Beetle, Tumblebug prefers to be called the Original Pooper Scooper. A garbage collector by day, he also enjoys sculpting.

Mosquito

Order: Diptera, Family: Culicidae

Only female mosquitoes prefer the blood of warm-blooded animals. Males feed on nectar and water.

Betty Skeeter lives in the Smith family backyard. When not baking cookies or volunteering, she likes to drink fresh blood.

Ladybug
(top of the pyramid)

Order: Coleoptera, Family: Coccinellidae

A farmer's best buddy, a ladybug can eat more than 5,000 plant-eating insects in its lifetime.

Ladybug, or Lady Beetle, divides her time between a regal windowsill and her winter home under a fallen tree.

Whirligig

Order: Coleoptera, Family: Gyrinidae

The whirligig has two pairs of eyes — one above and one below the water, providing views of both environments.

This water lover is a fan of water ballet. Whirligig's other passions include go-go dancing and canoeing.

Cricket

Order: Orthoptera, Family: Gryllidae

Male crickets can pitch chirps slightly higher than the highest octave on a piano.

Cricket is a celebrated singer of power ballads. He enjoys walks on the beach and quiet time spent with that "special green someone."